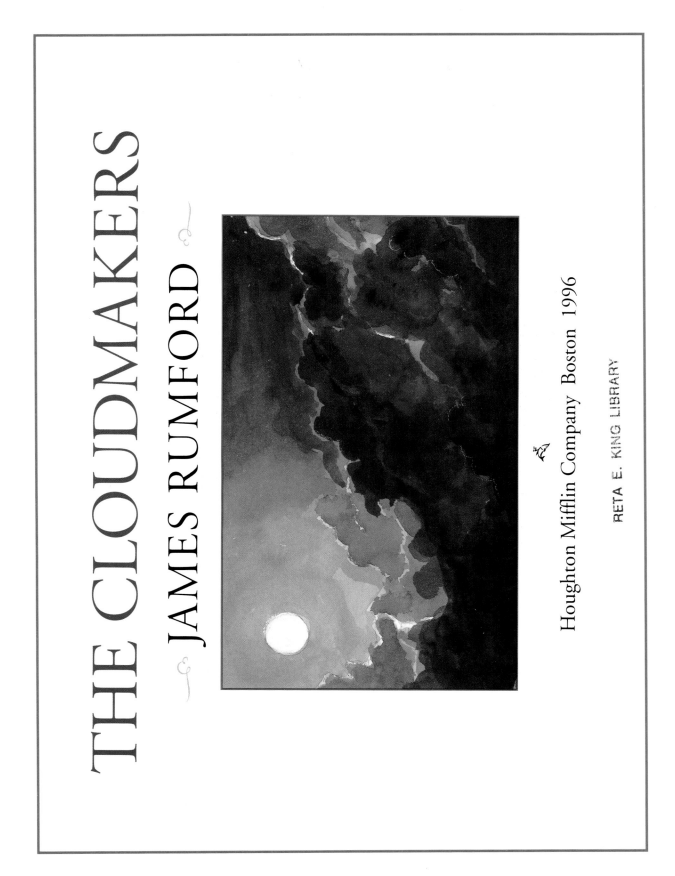

THE CLOUDMAKERS

JAMES RUMFORD

Houghton Mifflin Company Boston 1996

For information about this and other Houghton Mifflin
trade and reference books and multimedia products,
visit The Bookstore at Houghton Mifflin on the World Wide
Web at http://www.hmco.com/trade/.

Manufactured in the United States of America.

The text of this book is set in 16 pt. Adobe Garamond.

BVG 10 9 8 7 6 5 4 3 2 1

Library of Congress Cataloging-in-Publication Data

Rumford, James.

p.   cm.

Summary: A Chinese grandfather and his grandson who are captured
by the Arab army barter for their freedom by demonstrating the art of papermaking.

ISBN 0-395-76505-6

[1. Papermaking — Fiction. 2. Grandfathers — Fiction. 3. China — Fiction.]
I. Title.

PZ7.R8878Cl 1996   95-39998

[E] — dc20   CIP

                                                          AC

To Harriett Oberhaus

for her inspiration and encouragement

From beyond the Sky Mountains, almost beyond China itself, came an old Chinese grandfather and his grandson. In these troubled times of war, they were looking for work and had wandered long and far from their starving village.

"Grandpa," asked Young Wu, "how far is it to the next village?"

"Oh, I'm sure it's just over the next hill," said Grandfather Wu, trying not to make his voice sound as tired as his feet.

At the top of the next hill, grandfather and grandson stopped to rest. In the valley below, they could see a river and, in the distance, a village.

"Let's have a bit of rice cake," said Young Wu, trying not to make his voice sound as hungry as his stomach.

When they had eaten the tiny rice cake, Young Wu lay back against his grandfather and looked up at the clouds. "Tell me again, Grandpa, how do we make our special clouds?"

"Well," Grandfather said, beginning the story the way he always did, "making clouds begins with water."

Suddenly from the east came a great thundering of hooves as Chinese cavalrymen charged into the valley. From the west came a storm of Arab warriors to meet them. When the two armies clashed, grandfather and grandson hid their eyes. They did not see the Arab scouts coming up behind them. The Arabs seized them and took them to a prison camp crowded with defeated Chinese.

"Here comes our general with his lieutenant on the hill!" jeered one of the captured Chinese soldiers, for word of the old man and his son had quickly spread through the camp.

"General? Hah! He is just a starving peasant from the east, a tramp."

"My grandfather is not a tramp!" said Young Wu. "He can make clouds!"

The prisoners ignored him, turning away. The next day they were all to be sold into slavery.

In the morning, the Great Sultan from Samarkand arrived to select the best of the prisoners. When the guards brought grandfather and grandson before the Sultan, his counselors waved them away. Who would want an old man and a little boy?

With nothing to lose, Young Wu blurted out, "My grandfather can make clouds!" This caught the Sultan's attention and he turned to his interpreter, who explained. Grandfather and grandson trembled before the Great Sultan.

"If you can make clouds, make some now!" the Sultan ordered.

"These are special clouds," said Grandfather Wu. "It will take seven days to make them."

The Sultan thought for a moment. "Perhaps they are magicians. So be it! Seven days! Take them away!"

That night, under a bright moon, grandfather and grandson talked of the next seven days.

"But will the Sultan like our clouds?" asked Young Wu, looking up at the sky.

"I'm sure of it," said Grandfather, drifting off to sleep.

On the first of the seven days, Grandfather asked to go down to the river.

"Making clouds begins with water," shouted Young Wu to the guards.

Grandfather and grandson took off their shoes, which were made of hemp rope, and threw them into the pool near the river's edge. When the shoes were soaking wet, Grandfather pulled them out with his cane and slapped them down on a large flat rock. Then he began to beat them with his cane.

"This is thunder for our clouds," cried Young Wu.

The guards laughed. What a ridiculous sight! An old man beating his shoes until they fell apart!

On the second day, Grandfather collected ashes from the cook's fire. He put them in his empty carrying sack. Young Wu slowly poured boiling water over them. The water trickled through the sack and fell in drops into a large bowl.

"These are the stinging raindrops for our clouds!" proclaimed Young Wu.

On the third day, Grandfather boiled the beaten shoes

in the stinging rainwater.

"Look, billows of steam for our clouds!" shouted

Young Wu to the few onlookers.

By the fourth day, the hemp shoes had completely lost their shape, leaving strands of fiber. Grandfather fished the fibers out of the water, washed them, and put them in the sun. As soon as they were dry, Young Wu sprinkled them with water. All day long and for the next two days, they bleached the fibers.

On the morning of the seventh day, the strands of hemp were as white as clouds. Young Wu was exhausted.

A great crowd had gathered to see the "Chinese magicians." Grandfather and grandson approached the Sultan, where he sat eating fruit with his counselors.

Old Wu began to pound the white hemp with his cane. Then he set the soft fibers aside and broke the cane into four pieces, making a frame. He stretched a piece of his worn sack tightly over the frame, fastening it with string. He gave it to Young Wu, who held it high. "A net to catch our clouds!"

Now even the Sultan was laughing.

Grandfather called for a large tub of water. When the water was still, it reflected the blue sky. He put the beaten white fibers into the tub. They danced for a moment like clouds.

"Sorcerers!" The word ran in whispers through the crowd.

Grandfather now stirred the fibers in the tub and dipped the frame into the whirling water. He brought the frame up, shook it, and held it aloft. The crowd strained to see. The frame was covered in glistening white!

"A cloud!" Young Wu cried triumphantly.

The Sultan's chief counselor mocked, "That is no cloud!"

Calmly, Young Wu put the frame in the sun to dry. Soon Grandfather's magic would be let loose.

In a short time, the white pulp was dry. Just as Young Wu had pulled the cloud from the frame, a gust of wind snatched it from his fingers. It hovered before the Sultan, fluttering in the breeze. Then, lifeless, it floated to the ground. The crowd exploded with laughter.

"Silence!" shouted the Sultan. "A cloud this is not! But Chinese paper it surely is, for I have seen such a thing before." He turned to the old grandfather and grandson, "Can you show us the secrets of this art?"

"Yes, we can," said Young Wu, trying not to make his voice sound as proud as his heart.

"Then teach us this miracle."

And they did.

In Samarkand, Old Wu and Young Wu taught the people how to make paper. When they had showed them everything they knew, the Sultan gave them their freedom and filled their pockets with gold.

As Old Wu and Young Wu were leaving Samarkand, they looked back and saw the sky filled with clouds and the hills covered with paper.

In the year A.D. 751, the Chinese lost a battle on the banks of the Talas River as it flows into Kazakhstan from the Tian Shan or, as I have called them, the Sky Mountains. The victorious Arabs later claimed that they had captured several papermakers, whose names have unfortunately been lost to us. According to ancient Arab historians, these papermakers were taken to Samarkand, where they taught the people how to make paper. From Samarkand, papermaking slowly spread westward.

The Chinese, who invented paper over 2,000 years ago, often made it out of hemp. When they cooked the hemp, they added lye, which they made from wood ash and hot water, just as Grandfather Wu did when he made "stinging rainwater."

The Chinese, except in poetry, never referred to paper as "clouds." This was Grandfather Wu's way of adding a touch of magic to what is very hard work.